POSTMAN JOE

Story by Jane Pilgrim, illustrated by F. Stocks May

BROCKHAMPTON PRESS, LEICESTER

AND THE POTATO PRESS, CHICAGO

Published in 1973 in the United States of America by J. Philip O'Hara Inc,
Chicago and in Great Britain by Brockhampton Press Limited, Leicester
Published simultaneously in Canada by Van Nostrand Reinhold Limited, Scarborough, Ontario
This edition Copyright © Brockhampton Press 1973
Printed in Great Britain by Purnell and Sons Limited

Postman Joe was a bright, cheerful little robin who lived at Blackberry Farm. The farm people called him Postman Joe because he brought their letters (when there were any) and told them all the news. His real name was Joe Robin.

Joe Robin lived in an old kettle which someone, a
long time ago, had thrown into some bushes over the
wall at the bottom of the farmyard. He liked it very
much, and had made it nice and cosy with bits of
moss and horsehair. If he sat on the wall he could
see everything that happened at the farm, and
everyone knew where to find him.

Mrs. Squirrel was very friendly with Joe, because
they both understood about living in trees, and Joe
would often fly over to see Mrs. Squirrel and her
daughter Hazel. He would tell them where he had seen
a good crop of nuts, and they would tell him who had
gone down the lane below the big oak tree where
they lived.

One morning Mrs. Squirrel was in a great state of excitement. "You must fly up to the farm at once, Joe," she cried. "I have seen a Large Red Animal crawling up the lane, breathing out smoke. I'm sure it must be dangerous. Go and tell Mr. and Mrs. Smiles, and warn all the animals to stay at home to-day."

So Postman Joe flew off up to the farm, and there in
the yard was the Large Red Animal. But it was not
breathing out smoke now, it was standing quietly
outside the farm door. Mr. Smiles, the farmer, was
standing beside it, with Mrs. Smiles and Joy and Bob
(their children), and they all looked very pleased.

Bob saw Joe Robin flying carefully round, and he
called to him: "Come and look at our new tractor, Joe.
It is going to help Daddy do lots of work in the
fields, and when I'm big I'm going to learn to drive it."

Joe had never seen anything like it before, and he twittered with excitement as he looked at it. "I must go and tell the others!" he called; and he flew off to find Ernest Owl, who knew everything.

But Ernest Owl had never seen a tractor before,
either, and he told Joe he must fly round and make sure
that all the animals knew about it, so that they
would not be frightened. "It is your job as Postman
and Newsman to tell them," he hooted. "Mrs. Nibble
is sure to be upset if she sees a strange Red Monster
puffing into her field."

So Postman Joe went down to the field to tell Mrs. Nibble first. "Don't worry, Mrs. Nibble," he said. "There is nothing to be frightened about. It is only a sort of large new animal to help Mr. Smiles in the fields. But we thought you ought to know before you met it. I'm going round to tell all the others."

And he flew off round the farm. All day he spent
explaining about the Large Red Animal which had
come to live at Blackberry Farm, and everyone was
very excited and very glad that Joe Robin had
brought the news to them. "Thank you, Joe," Henry
the Pig grunted. "I don't know what we should
do without you."

By evening Joe was tired, and he was glad when he
perched again on the wall beside his house. It had
been a busy day, but it had been a good one and he
had passed on this exciting news to all the animals.
That was his job, and he had done it. Ernest Owl
would be pleased.

Ernest Owl was pleased. And he flew down late in the evening to tell him so. "You've done well, Joe Robin," he hooted. "Now we must just arrange a meeting to welcome this Large Red Animal. I have written some notes, and I want you to take them round to-morrow."

So the next morning Joe Robin got out his postman's bag, put in Ernest Owl's notes, and flew off round the farm and the fields.

Some of the animals could not read; so Joe Robin
read aloud to Little Martha the Lamb, Walter Duck,
and George the Kitten: "Come to the yard after tea
to meet the Large Red Animal. Signed, Ernest Owl."

So after tea the animals gathered round the Large Red
Animal in the yard, and Joe Robin perched bravely on its
chimney (which wasn't smoking!) and Ernest Owl spoke out:
"Welcome to Blackberry Farm, Large Red Animal, and thank
you, Joe Robin, for bringing us together and telling us
all about it." And Joe Robin felt he was a very important
person at Blackberry Farm, and he was very proud.